Dedicated to all those folks who give more than they take

Also published by Ruwanga Trading:

Happy as a Dolphin
The Goodnight Gecko
The Whale Who Wanted to be Small
The Wonderful Journey
A Whale's Tale
The Gift of Aloha
The Shark Who Learned a Lesson
Gecko Hide and Seek
The Brave Little Turtle
Tikki Turtle's Quest

First published 2010 by Ruwanga Trading
ISBN 978-0970152831
Printed in China by Everbest Printing Co., Ltd.

BOOK ENQUIRES AND ORDERS:
Booklines Hawaii, a division of The Islander Group
269 Pali'i Street
Mililani, Hawaii, 96789
Phone: 808-676-0116, ext.206
Fax: 808-676-5156
Toll Free: 1-877-828-4852
Website: www.islandergroup.com

How The Geckos Learned to Chirp

Written by Terry and Tara McBarnet

Illustrated by DongA

Happiness is not something you search for...
It is something you do and it will find you

Long ago when the world was new, Hawaii was already beautiful. The trees were laden with fruit and flowers, and turquoise waves tumbled toward the golden beaches. The wind whispered softly through the ferns and twittering bird songs filled the day. At night the stars sparkled in the clear sky and the warm air was quiet... very quiet... because the geckos had not yet learned to chirp.

The geckos lived next to a stream in a young koa tree, and they were grumpy from the moment they woke up, all through the day. They only spoke if they were complaining about something, and they were not at all nice to each other. Everyday they grumbled how hard their lives were and how they wished their lives were different so they could be happy.

One day a new little creature came to the koa tree. "Hello, my name is Pono. What are your names?" he asked with a friendly smile. The geckos weren't nice to each other and they sure weren't going to be nice to a stranger. After a rude silence, one of them finally asked, "Why are you here and why do you have such funny looking spots?" "This is my new home, and I love my spots. My Mom and Dad gave them to me," the little creature replied.

Day after day, and night after night Pono lived cheerfully alongside the grumpy geckos. He would smile and whistle quietly all day long. Pono's cheerfulness bothered the geckos so much that they stopped being grumpy with each other and instead directed all their grumpiness to Pono.

"Don't you know we don't like you and we think you are ugly?" said one gecko unkindly.

"I'm sorry you're unhappy," replied Pono. "But I can't help showing how much I love my new home! Aren't we so lucky to live in such a beautiful tree?"

"Beautiful tree? Our tree is so useless; it has no flowers like the ohia tree... or fruit like the papaya tree. It's not fair that the birds have everything. We've got nothing but this silly little tree," they grumbled.

"It might be little, but it's a strong tree with all we need to eat and drink" Pono replied, cheerfully sipping a dewdrop from a nearby leaf. A gecko snapped up a mosquito, and greedily licked his lips.

Days went by and Pono continued his happy ways, quietly whistling cheerfully while he went about his daily business. The grumpy geckos were annoyed but curious that he carried himself in this way.

As it began to lightly rain, one of the geckos asked, "Why are you so happy?"

Pono answered, "Our lives are precious, and every day is special to me. I wish you would also enjoy every day you have in our beautiful tree."

"Hampff..." said the geckos because they were confused, and they sneered, "How can any day be special if it rains? The rain makes us cold and miserable."

"The rain satisfies our thirst and keeps our tree green," Pono replied with a smile, "and besides, I'm always busy so I never seem to feel the cold."

Whenever they treated him badly, Pono would say, "I'm not going to waste my time getting angry, and I'm sure not going to let you hurt my feelings. Just because you have decided to be unhappy doesn't mean that I must also become unhappy." With that he'd get back to work, whistling cheerfully and with a smile on his face.

One night the clouds moved in and the wind began to blow very hard. The little koa tree was shaking and tossing about, and then the storm really came and it started raining harder than it had ever rained before. "FLASH" went the lightning, streaking across the black and stormy sky. "Ka-BOOM!" went the thunder, making the ground shake and every little creature on the koa tree tremble.

There had never been a storm like this before, and the geckos crawled about for cover, fighting and shouting at one another as they tried to hold onto the strongest branch or leaf they could find. The koa tree was bent over by the force of the wind, but it stayed firmly rooted and all the little geckos were terrified as they hung on for dear life. "Help us!" they screamed into the dark sky, as the water in the stream rose higher and higher and threatened to wash them and the little tree away.

The wind howled, the rain flooded down from an angry sky and the geckos whimpered in terror, clawing at one another as they tried to get to the top of the tree. In the middle of the fury of the storm they heard whistling that got louder and louder until it burst into a mighty whistle.

The whistle was so pure and so powerful that it rose above the roar of the storm. "That has to be Pono," said one of the geckos. "Let's go see," said another. The geckos crawled towards the sound and there was Pono, whistling a wonderful tune and not looking at all scared. In fact, he was smiling and seemed to be having the time of his life as he gripped on tightly, with all his might.

"We're going to die!" screamed the geckos and they were surprised when Pono turned to them and said in a strong voice, "Hang on tightly, believe in yourself, help your friends, and we will all get through this storm. You geckos are bigger and stronger than I am so why are you scared?" The geckos hung on tightly like Pono, comforted by his powerful whistle.

"Show us how to whistle," the geckos called to Pono. Pono showed them but every time they tried to whistle, all they were able to make was a chirping sound. "Chirp-chirp" went the geckos, and "Oh no, we can't whistle!"

"That's perfect," said Pono. "I wish I could chirp like you!"

The geckos were so pleased with themselves. They looked at one another proudly, and one or two little chirps soon became many big chirps, as they chirped with all their hearts. The stormy night was filled with gecko's chirping and Pono's mighty whistle.

By the next day the storm had passed, leaving many fallen trees behind. The geckos were feeling quite different. They were happy to be alive. Their island... the little koa tree... the birds... everything looked so good. They were so happy they were even polite to each other. Pono was their hero. He had got them safely through the storm. That night the koa tree rang out with cheerful chirping. Life was very good.

Happy days were followed by happy weeks and the geckos loved their new life. Everybody was polite and helpful to each other.

Pono loved his friends and they looked up to him. During the day the island buzzed with cheerful sounds and beautiful chirping carried the night. The geckos had decided to make the best of their lives. Pono was very proud of his friends.

One day Pono started spinning a cocoon with a silky thread that seemed to shimmer in the sunlight. He smiled sweetly as he quietly whistled away, but the geckos noticed that he was slowing down. "What is wrong Pono? Can we help?" They asked kindly. "Nothing is wrong my friends, I'm just feeling a little tired," said Pono. "I think the time has come for me to move onto my next life."

The geckos were scared. They said, "You can't leave us. We'll be sad and not able to carry on without you."

Pono looked fondly at his friends. "During the storm you didn't think that you could continue, but look how strong and happy you are today. My time has come and I must go, but I will always be close by."

"Find comfort in the leaves that shelter you by day and the stars that come out at night. Your good life will continue because you have decided to be happy and to care for each other, so nothing can take that away from you. All I ask is for you to chirp at night so I will know that you are fine." Night came, and the geckos chirped with all their hearts.

The next morning when dawn brushed the leaves with a pink glow, Pono was gone. In his place was a hard shell hanging from a twig. The geckos were sad. They missed Pono, but when they thought of what their happy friend had taught them, they felt better. Days went by, with the geckos being kind and helpful to all the other creatures in the koa tree.

Then one morning, the shell was empty...

Pono had moved on to another life, and although the gecko's eyes filled with tears, they were grateful to have had such a loving and happy friend come into their lives. They would always miss Pono, but in their hearts they knew he would always be nearby. To celebrate his happy spirit they still to this day, chirp at night to tell Pono that everything is fine and that life is a wonderful miracle.